Fresh Fish Tales

If you read to me,
one day I'll be able to read to you!

Dedication

Reading to my nieces and nephews and making up stories was oh so much fun! We are all familiar with the saying, "I could write a book." The question is always when. This book has been in the making for over forty years. Having recently retired, I've decided now is the time. So, with lots of love and good wishes for their futures, I dedicate this book to:

My niece and nephews:
Leah, Donovan, Kent II, and LeByron;

My great-nieces and -nephews:
Aniyah, Ariana, Jada, Sunday, Amir, LeByron Jr., Jayln, and Jordan;

My great-great-niece and -nephew:
Audrey and Shane;

And to all children who hold the power in their little hands
to help make this world a better place.

Fresh Fish Tales
Copyright © 2024 Berita Martin

All rights reserved.

No part of this publication in print or in electronic format may be reproduced, stored in a retrieval system, or transmitted in any form or by any means, electronic, mechanical, photocopying, recording, or otherwise without the prior written permission of the publisher. This is a work of fiction. Names, characters, organizations, places, events and incidents are either the products of the author's imagination or are used fictitiously. Any resemblance to actual persons, living or dead, or actual events is purely coincidental.

Text and illustrations by Berita Martin
Editing, design, distribution by Bublish

ISBN: 978-1647048-99-0 (hardcover)
ISBN: 978-1647048-98-3 (eBook)

This book belongs to

_______________________________________.

(Write your name here.)

Fresh Fish Tales

All the fish in the ocean and all the creatures in the sea are as varied in their differences as you and me.

But . . . some things we have in common—some things are the same. We feel the same happiness, we feel the same pain, we breathe in the air around us, we wish upon a star, so . . . why can we not accept each other just the way we are? This is the basic premise for **Fresh Fish Tales**.

Utilizing the alphabet letters A to O, different kinds of fish and sea creatures share their stories "tales" in rhythmic phrasing and rhyme. The tales deal with topics such as: self-esteem, love, family and friends, responsibility and more. Volume two, P to Z is a future project.

Meet Our Fish Friends!

Angelfish

One of the most beautiful and highly colored fishes are angelfish. Domestic angelfish come in almost every color of the rainbow. They are found mostly on the reefs of the Atlantic, Indian, and Pacific Oceans.

ANGEL THE ANGELFISH

Angel was a fish who wished and wished and wished. He wished
he were a bird, a snail, just anything but a fish!

He felt that other creatures were more interesting.
All he did was swim around in the sea.

He said to his mother, "Mommy, please! Why must we be
fish swimming in the sea?"

Angel's mother was very wise. She smiled and looked into his big
fish eye. She explained, "Everyone and everything has its place and
time to be.

Some may be birds,
some may be trees,
but our time for now, Angel dear, is here in the sea.

Be proud of what you are, Angel, swim straight and fast and free.
Be the best little angelfish that you can possibly be."

Barracuda

The barracuda is one of the most dangerous fish of the sea. They have two rows of razor-sharp teeth! They are found in subtropical and tropical oceans.

BENNY BARRACUDA

Benny Barracuda took a trip to Bermuda. His doctor felt the change would do him good. He had been so sad. He had been so blue. Poor Benny didn't know what to do! For Benny was in love with Betty, she was his love so true. But… Betty did not return his love, which left Benny feeling bluer than blue. Benny said to the doctor, "Doctor, I cannot see why Betty's heart is not filled with love for me. I send her gifts, I sing her songs, I pour my heart out to her all the day long."

The doctor said to Benny, "I guess we can't always pick the one we love and expect them to come along. Benny, you've done nothing wrong, for love makes and sings it's very own song.

Love is a mystery and a magic to behold. But when two hearts share it, it's worth far more than gold. My advice to you is simply get away! Clear your head, dry your eyes, and save your heart for another day. For that day will come, Benny. You won't know when, you won't know where, but one day you'll turn around and love will be there."

Codfish

Codfish are found in the Atlantic and Pacific Oceans. They feed on crabs and shrimp and most anything. They are very slow swimmers. But they can travel up to 200 miles to reach their breeding grounds. Females can lay up to five million eggs!

CONNIE CODFISH

Connie Codfish craved crayfish, shellfish, and clams. She cried, "Curtis, my husband, catch them faster if you can! You know I am full with eggs and I must eat—I MUST!"

Curtis said, "Connie, my cutie, don't make such a fuss, for I have gone to the market and brought home a bus. A bus full of crayfish and shellfish and such. So eat all you want, eat all you may, for you will still have shellfish to eat another day!"

Dolphins

Dolphins are marine mammals found in both warm and cold coastal waters. They also live in deep oceans far from the coastline. Dolphins are very intelligent and can learn many tricks!

DELILAH AND DANNY DOLPHIN

Delilah and Danny Dolphin lived in the sea. They loved
their beautiful home, they loved living free.
One day while swimming, Delilah was caught in a net!
Danny said, "Don't fret, Delilah, dearest, they haven't got you yet!"
Danny swam for help, pleading with everyone in sight.
Until he came upon a swordfish, who gave him such a fright!
"Oh please, Mr. Swordfish, I'd give my life to thee
if only you would help set my poor Delilah free."
So they swam to Delilah and Mr. Swordfish cut her free!
And then . . . a most amazing thing happened.
Mr. Swordfish told them to flee!
He said, "Danny, you are truly devoted and I cannot harm thee,
for the love you share is far too rare for it to end by me."

Eels

Eels are ray-finned fish that have wormlike bodies. There are about 800 species of eels. They are found in freshwater and saltwater throughout the world. Some eels are electric and some have needle-sharp teeth!

ENRIQUE THE EEL

Enrique the eel could make you squeal when he sang his eely tunes.
He was suave and debonair with big black hair.
When he wiggled on the stage, everyone would stare

All the girls loved him!
Couldn't get enough of him and cried,
"Enrique, please sing us a tune!"
He sang high.
He sang low.
He even sang sta-cca-to.

Talent scouts have come to hear
him croon. They say he'll be in
the movies soon.
And now you know the story of an eel,
his hair, and glory.
He is Enrique! A talented singer,
that's a Moray!
Ask him and he will sing for you!

Flounders

Flounders are a flatfish species that have both eyes on top of their heads! The underside of a flounder is flat and solid white. They spend their entire life on the bottom of the sea.

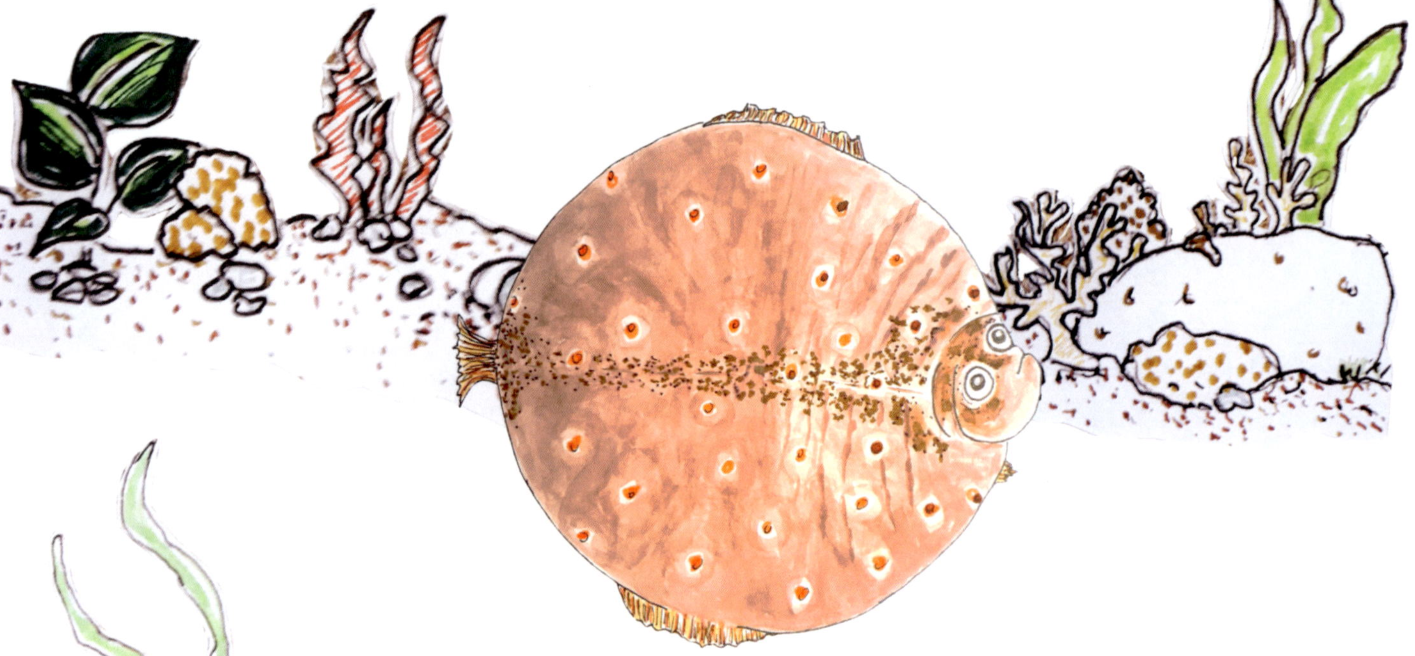

FRANKIE FLOUNDER

If little Frankie Flounder gets any rounder, he won't be able to fit into his fin! A flatfish fin goes on top, you know.

But Frankie got so round, it looked as if he were about to blow! His mother would say, "Frankie, please go out and play. Don't just swim around the house and eat all day!"

What Frankie needed was a friend, someone who would play
with him. But all of Frankie's friends were far away, for Frankie's
family had moved to a new town, and there were no other little fish
around. So Frankie stayed home and ate all day.

One day his father said, "Frankie, I want you to meet Fernando.
His parents just bought the house next door."

Frankie looked at Fernando. Fernando looked at Frankie and from
that moment on, they were inseparable. All day every day they
would swim and play.

Sometimes his mother would call out, "Lunchtime!
Don't you want to eat today?"

Then something wonderful happened. Frankie began to flatten.
He got into shape and he felt great.

When asked what lesson he had learned, Frankie did reply,
"Friends and fun and exercise will help make you healthy
and wise."

Frankie and Fernando are still the best of friends.

Grunt Fish

The Grunt fish family is one of the most numerous of all tropical fishes. The name is due to the fact that it has the ability to make a deep, muffled grunting sound, which can be heard some distance above water!

GRIZELLA GRUNT

Grizella Grunt performed stunts as the feature star of the fish follies. She had grace, she had poise, but she made a lot of noise, for she grunted with each and every volley.

She swam up. She swam down. She did flip-flops all around, and with each toss and turn she would resound!

"My, my, she would cry. Such a noisy fish am I. But there's simply nothing I can do! They hear me from above, they hear me from below, for my grunts do tend to echo, you know.

Oh, what shall I do?"
She thought for a moment and then said, "I know—I'll speak with the Great Wallou. She is the wisest creature in the ocean, and she'll know what to do!"

Grizella went to the Great Wallou and indeed she told Grizella exactly what to do.

Her next performance was at nine and she made it back just in time.

As the spotlight came up, Grizella performed a most daring triple belly flip-flop and from deep within her came the LOUDEST GRUNT EVER!

The crowd was stunned . . . not a sound came from anyone . . . and Grizella feared her career was done. Then . . . one by one, a chant had begun until it got louder and louder, which made Grizella prouder and prouder. "Grizella is the greatest, Grizella is the greatest!" came from the lips of each and every one. Then Grizella knew the words of the Great Wallou were true, for she had told her, "Your grunts are a part of you, and if you are ashamed of them, others will be too. Never be ashamed of who you are."

Headfish

They are also called ocean sunfish. Headfish have leathery skin and appear to be all head and no tail! They live at around 2,000 feet deep and are found in the Atlantic, Pacific, and Indian Oceans. Headfish can live up to one hundred years and their weight ranges from 500 to 2,000 pounds. When the ocean is cold, they float close to the surface to sunbathe, which raises their body temperature. Headfish can also leap up to ten feet in the air!

HADLEY HEADFISH

Hadley Headfish was heading for Hawaii when suddenly he had quite a thought. Wouldn't it be nice if we were a horde of headfish heading for that lovely vacation spot?

So he called his uncles, Harry and Hal.
He called his aunts, Henrietta and Hallie.
He called his twin cousins, the Halibuts.

All were packed and ready to go
when Hadley cried out, "Cheerio!" and
they headed for the islands beyond the horizon.

There was surfing, there was sun,
Uncle Harry even hulaed some!
A grand time was had by everyone.

Hadley was happy they all had come.
But it burdened his heart to leave everyone.
Packing to go home made him glum.

Hadley thought, how can I keep the family happy?
Then . . . Hadley had a plan.
Indeed the plan was grand. He announced it
that night at the luau.

"Attention, everyone! Vacation time is done.
We've all had so much fun.
To keep in touch with those we love so dear,
let us meet again in Bermuda next year!"

So from that time on, when winter winds would come,
Hadley Headfish and his family would head for the sun.

Indian Fish

The Red Indian fish is a member of the Australian prowfishes. It is also known as the red forehead fish and is an uncommon species. It has a compressed body and long dorsal fin, which resembles an indigenous North American chief's headdress. It is known to periodically shed its skin in one piece!

LITTLE BIG CHIEF
RED INDIAN FISH

Little Big Chief Red Indian Fish was as brave as brave can be. All the little fish looked up to him, and he helped the elderly.

One day a school of bully fish came swimming into town.
They were mean and nasty and yelled a lot and threw their
weight around.

A committee was formed, and these fish were warned to
shape up or get out of town!
The bully fish declined and instead made up their minds to
perform all kinds of dastardly deeds.

The town was in trouble; yes, they needed help on the
double.
They cried, "Who will save us from bullies such as these?"
An envoy was sent to get Little Big Chief Red Indian Fish and
to inform him what was going down.

When the chief arrived, he called the bullies outside. They
met him with their snickers and their grins. Chief said, "Boys,
I hear you're makin' a lot of noise, and we don't cotton to that
in this here town. So pack up your fins before real trouble
begins, cause I'm the roughest ray-finned fish around!"

They laughed and they howled. Chief began to scowl.

Then . . . he did a little dance, which put them all into a
trance.
When they awoke, they were in the next town! "Wow! What
just happened?

We didn't even see his fins a-flappin'," cried the bullies.

"One thing, for sure, we'd hate to see him when he is really
sore. We'll never go back to his town no more!"

Jambeau

Jambeau is a member of the spikefish family. They are usually found in coral bottoms of the Florida Keys and the Gulf of Mexico. They come in a wide variety of shapes, colors, and sizes.

JENNY JAMBEAU

Jenny Jambeau was a coral beauty who lived in the Florida Keys.

She was dainty and cute and looked great in her fish suit,
but she was as stuck-up as a fish could be!

Bragging to the town as she swam around, "How wonderful
it is to be me!"

She was pretty saucy and very bossy, always demanding
instead of asking and saying please.

Her parents allowed her to travel, and she would babble
and babble, about how she went to Aruba and swam
around Cuba.

She traveled with a school and thought she was cool. So
selfish a fish was she!

Always first in line.
Always first to say, "Mine!"
Jenny's good manners were very hard to find.
Never gracious, polite, courteous, or kind.

On one sunny day, Jenny did spy a beautiful lure that
caught her eye. Jenny Jambeau said, "I want it! That should
be mine!"

She clamped down on the lure and was snatched up for
sure by a fisherman on the sea.

No one could dispute that Jenny was cute.
Now she looks good on that plaque—
at Joe's Seafood Shack!

Killifish

There are thousands of species of killifish. Some are also known as mummichogs. Most are small colorful fish that have an unusual upright jumping ability, which enables them to maneuver on land and find water. Once on land, they use their tails to jump inches into the air! Killifish can breathe air through their skin.

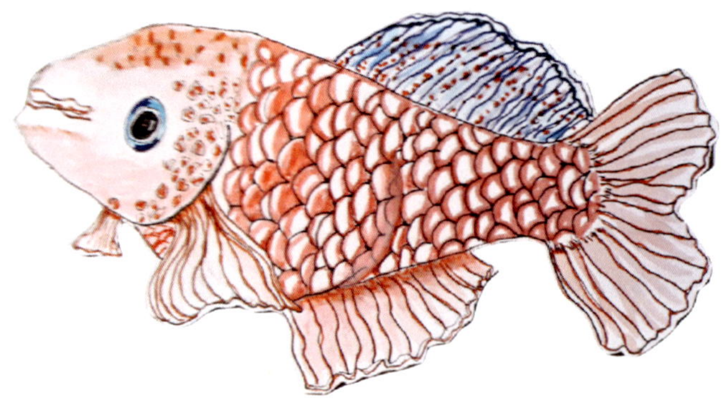

KENNY KILLIFISH

Kenny Killifish was quite a handsome dish, and females would come from miles around. During breeding season, he was one gorgeous reason to get married and settle down.

He had a killer smile and a devastating style that would lure all the girls to him.

But the thing that made Kenny really great, his heart was as big as the Golden Gate. To the sweet and demure he would gravitate.

He fell in love with Ella and he became her fella, which made the other girls green with envy. They'd say, "Why, she's no beauty. She's not even a cutie. She's dull and plain and gray."

But Kenny, being a kind fellow, would never listen to them bellow. He said, "I love my Ella anyway."

For you see . . . Kenny was not merely handsome on the outside, he was handsome through and through, with an eye that saw beauty in the things that others do. No, Ella was not a beauty like all the rest, but she had a heart that none other possessed.

Louvar

Also known as a surgeonfish, Louvar have heads that look like dolphins and the body shape of a tuna. This is a rare fish and not many have been caught. They live in the tropical and subtropical waters of all oceans. Large females can produce a huge number of eggs. It was recorded that a five-foot-long female had up to forty-seven million eggs!

LEONARD LOUVAR

Leonard Louvar was a lovely lad who would brighten the hearts of the very sad. Always helpful and kind, he even whistled all the time. He was growing up to be just like his dad.

A true friend was he when one was in need. Never cross or mean or mad. When asked how he became that way, Leonard would always smile and say, "I guess I was just born that way!"

His mom and dad were grateful for everything they had. They would say, "Do your best, whatever the test, and don't give in too quickly. Remember, a friend is rare so always take care to treat them properly."

"I guess," Leonard would say, "what I've been taught along the way is to give with a smile and it will come back to you someday."

Molly Miller

Molly millers are also called blennies. They are small fish with elongated bodies and large lips. Above its eyes are fuzzy eyebrows! They are found in the western Atlantic waters and are great utility fish because they eat algae in fish tanks. Molly millers are reportedly clever, excitable, and scrappy.

MILD MOLLY MILLER

Mild Molly Miller never put up a fuss. She would even let others swim before her while getting on the bus.

She was timid. She was shy. She was very insecure. When in a crowd of fish, she was even more demure.

When her parents were away, Aunt Mildred came to stay. She noticed that Molly would not go out to play. That made her auntie say, "Why are you so bashful? Why are you so shy? Why can't you smile and look other fish in the eye?"

With a tear and a sigh, Molly did reply, "Auntie . . . something is wrong, I've known it all along. Everything is blurry and so unclear. It makes me self-conscious and nervous, I fear."

Auntie said, "Molly girl, you need glasses! My friend, Dr. Cuatro Ojos, makes glasses for the masses.

You will make a splash with better vision. You will be brave and confident too! Take it from your auntie—I wear glasses too!"

Needlefish

Needlefish are also called garfish or long jaws. They have itchy bellies due to small parasites that attach themselves to their skin. To get rid of the parasites, needlefish will jump over anything that will scrape their bellies! They often leap over small boats rather than go around them. Their long, narrow jaws and sharp teeth can be dangerous.

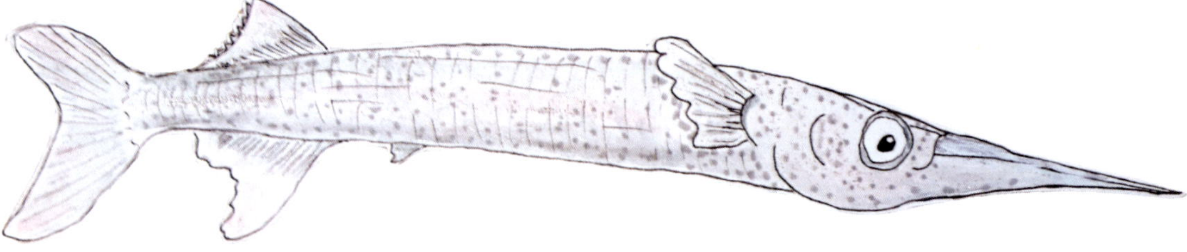

NEDDY NEEDLEFISH

For the first time Needy Needlefish and his little sis Tish were going to be left home alone. Said Tish to Neddy, "We can play with Teddy and have tea and crumpets and scones!"

Neddy's mom and dad were really glad to have a date night where they could be alone. The Needlefish left, putting Neddy to the test. This would be his first chance to guppy-sit on his own.

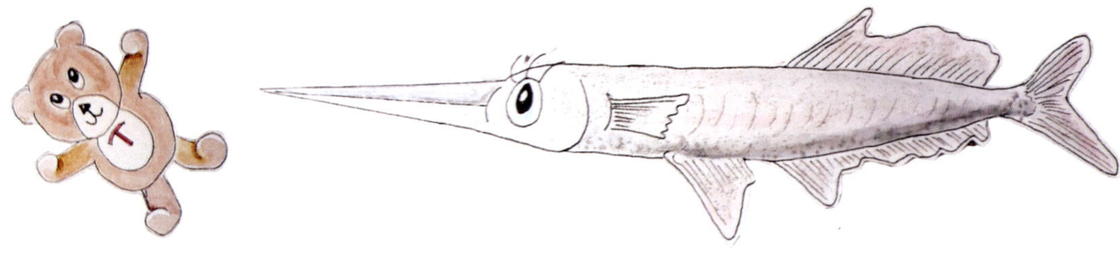

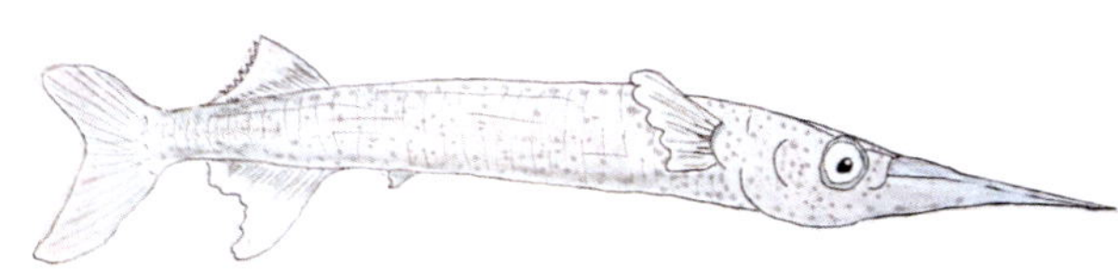

As soon as they left, wouldn't you guess, Tish began to cry
and moan. Neddy said, "I'm ready. Let's play with Teddy."
But Tish said, "No! Leave me alone."

Neddy turned his back—now why did he do that, because
Tish swam right out the door! When he turned around, she…
nowhere to be found. Needy knew he would have to track
her down.

He was responsible for Tish. No matter how hard he
wished, she would never behave when mom and dad
weren't at home.

He searched next door . . . he searched at the store . . . he even
swam all the way to the shore! No luck there, so he tried Fish
Square, but Tish could not be found.

He was getting frantic, and he just about panicked when he
saw mom and dad swimming home. He had to find Tish and
in a hurry! He said, "I can't go back alone."

And find her he did, with the help of a squid. He grabbed
her fin, and she swam with him as fast as the current
would let them.

What a brat she had been. Guppy-sitting was not for him.
Such a naughty and insolent fish. What a chore to watch
little Tish!

Old Spot

Also known as the spot croaker, Virginia spot, and Norfolk spot, the spot is a species of short-lived saltwater fish. Its most distinguishing characteristic is the dark spot that appears behind each gill.

OLD SPOT

It was a bright and beautiful day when Old Spot passed away. Friends came from far and near to give one last and final cheer.

He will truly be missed. He will surely be mourned, but the memory of Old Spot will forever live on.

He was a friend to all, selfless though small. Always ready to lend a helping fin. Before he passed, he chiseled on brass a few words of wisdom for us all.

This is his prayer, this is his wish, that he will forever be remembered for this:

Love is expressed in many ways. It may be a touch, it may be a deed, it may be a gaze. Show your love. Choose your way. Speak up now while you may. Memories are powerful and they do live on. Leave happy memories of your days in the sun. On this occasion of my passing, my last wish is for all to swim side by side, fin to fin. Let your family and friends know how much you love them. Let them know today while their gills still breathe. For tomorrow may be too late and then you'll grieve. Tell them now before they go, you will take comfort in knowing you told them so. Nam-myoho-renge-kyo.

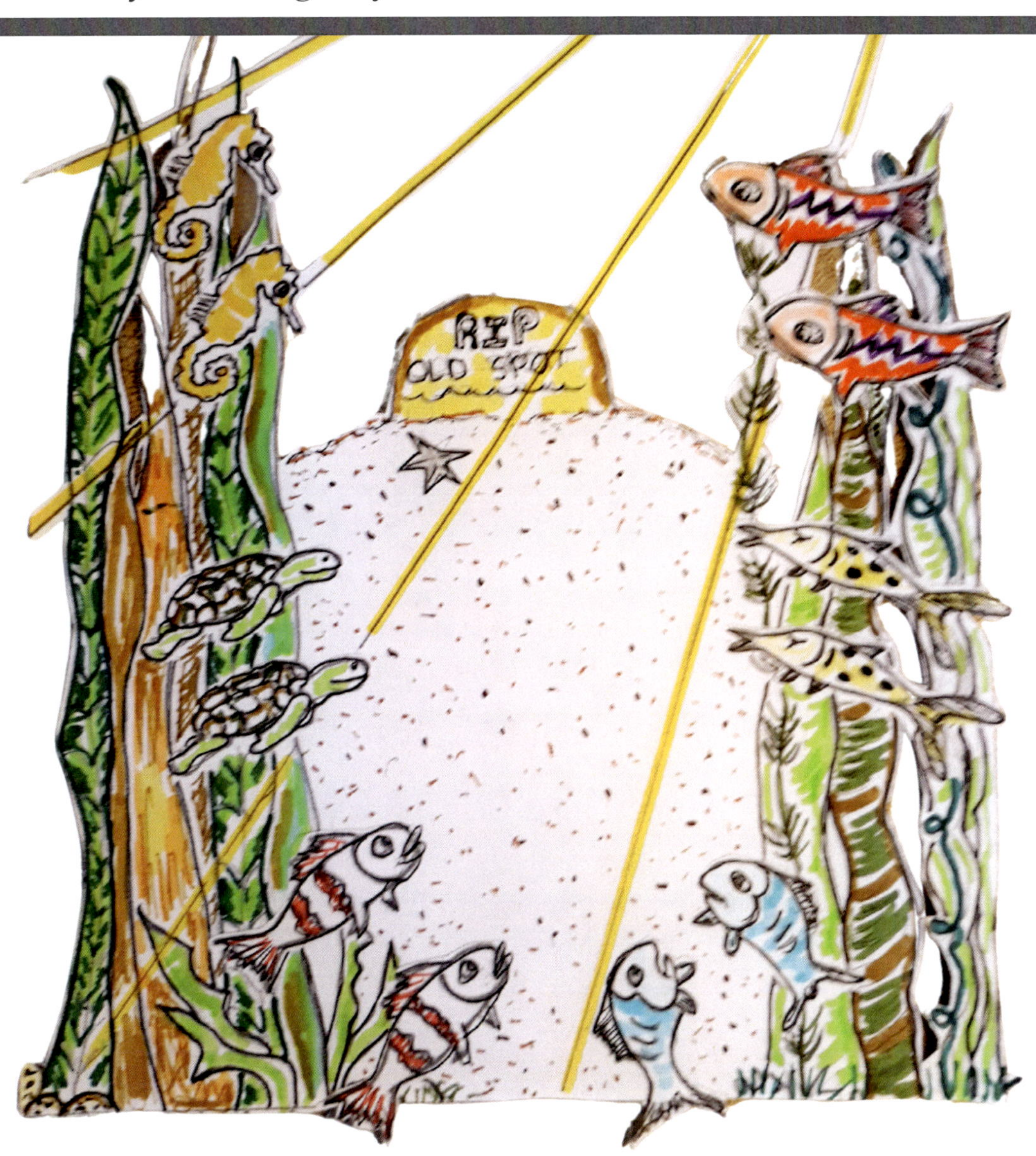

EPILOGUE

You have met different kinds of fish and sea creatures, and they have shared their tales in rhyme. What lessons have you learned from them? How will you use what they learned in your life?

To find a secret message, answer the following questions. Write the first letter of the answer on the line next to each question to solve this puzzle. If you do this every day, this good deed will come back to you!

~ Which story is about love and heartbreak? _____

~ Which story is about popularity and
   self-assurance? _____

~ Which story is about inner beauty
   versus outer beauty? _____

~ Which story is about bullying? _____

~ Which story is about responsibility? _____

~ Which story is about sacrifice and mercy? _____

BERMUDA

www.ingramcontent.com/pod-product-compliance
Lightning Source LLC
Chambersburg PA
CBRC101118300726
48981CB00012B/470